Forever Connected

Adventures and Activities with Grandchildren

Linda Chiara

This publication is designed to provide accurate and authoritative information in regard to the subject matter covered. It is sold with the understanding that neither the author nor the publisher is engaged in rendering legal, investment, accounting or other professional services. While the publisher and author have used their best efforts in preparing this book, they make no representations or warranties with respect to the accuracy or completeness of the contents of this book and specifically disclaim any implied warranties of merchantability or fitness for a particular purpose. No warranty may be created or extended by sales representatives or written sales materials. The advice and strategies contained herein may not be suitable for your situation. You should consult with a professional when appropriate. Neither the publisher nor the author shall be liable for any loss of profit or any other commercial damages, including but not limited to special, incidental, consequential, personal, or other damages.

Contents

Introduction 1

1. Newborns to Toddler 6
2. Toddler and Preschool Age 13
3. Winter and/or Christmas Crafts - Preschool to Early Elementary 30
4. Elementary Age 35
5. Preteens and Teens 50
6. Long Distance Grandparenting 73
7. My Final Suggestion 98

About the author 100

Introduction

From the moment our grandchildren are born, we are putty in their hands.

Of course, we felt the same way when our own children were born, but there was such an enormous amount of responsibility that came with being a new parent. Our time was no longer our own and we didn't know all the things we thought we should. Plus, we felt compelled to do *everything* right.

As they grew, we shuffled between our jobs, our children's never-ending school, sports, and social activities, in addition to keeping up with our regular daily chores of laundry, cooking, cleaning, car maintenance, and yard work.

> *We didn't have the time to savor our babies the way we would have liked.*

When a grandchild comes along, however, we are often in a place in life where our time is ours and we can spend it as we want.

We have a wealth of knowledge, an abundance of unique skills and the yearning to become the grandparents we dreamed we might become someday when our children were young.

If you were lucky enough to have wonderful grandparents, or if your children had fantastic grandparents, you know what a blessing it is. And if you didn't have either wonderful grandparents or if your children missed out on having fantastic grandparents, you now have the opportunity to give your grandkids what you always wished had been available to you.

We want to provide our grandchildren with joyous and delightful memories, and we have a world of possibilities to do so. Our job as grandparents is to love those children with all our hearts and be the best influence that we possibly can be. And there are few endeavors that provide as much satisfaction as the pleasure life with grandchildren can bring.

Our patience is valued beyond words. And we *are* more patient. We are not thrown by messy spills or middle school drama because we are painfully aware that those little spills and messes and the heartache of a preteen drama are over way too soon.

And let's not forget about how your presence and influence can enrich the lives of *your* children (the parents of your little sweethearts). They also get something out of having a handy-dandy grandparent to help out. They get the best of both worlds; extra hearts loving their offspring and a break from the daily persistent busyness that occurs when children join the household.

You are useful and needed. By getting involved in your grandchildren's lives you are giving them the benefit of your expertise. And it doesn't take much. You don't need any particular skill set, (although if you have a skill set to pass on, great) and you don't need to break the bank to make them happy.

But what if you are a grandparent who lives so far away that you cannot be involved in the day-to-day aspects of your family's lives? How can you be a good and positive influence on your grandchildren, if the majority of the time that you spend with them is on FaceTime?

Fear not! If you are one of the grandparents who live far away from your grandkids, please don't despair. I have a chapter for long distance grandparenting which goes miles beyond Facetime. No doubt you are wishing you could do more. You can! And I will show you how.

It's all about connection. And connection doesn't require a lot of money or close physical distance.

What it does require is a little thought, patience, and the understanding that the world is different today than it was when we were young. Let go of what you thought being a grandparent should be and grab onto what it is today, in today's world with this new generation.

> *Forever Connected is much more than a book. It is an exploration and a guide for creating solid and enduring relationships by offering helpful and entertaining suggestions and activities that foster and produce a deep and positive relationship between two generations that will benefit both.*

My hope is that you will do the activities that appeal to you and which suit your availability, capability and lifestyle. With each new page, you'll be shown countless ways that these unique connections can be fostered.

Whether you start a new hobby together or share an old favorite, go on day trips, or create an arts and crafts center for them to explore when they spend the night, it doesn't matter.

The point is to be with them in the moment, so that you can both listen and learn from one another. Because if you are listening, you will learn as much from your grandchildren as they will from you. And you will become an everlasting and cherished memory that they will look back on when they are grandparents themselves.

So if you're a new grandparent looking to embark on an unforgettable journey with your grandchildren or if you've been a grandparent for a while and are seeking new ways to bond with them, this book is the perfect companion.

Let it inspire you to make every moment count and create lifelong memories that will keep you *forever connected*.

Chapter One

Newborns to Toddler

This will be the shortest chapter because the best you can do for the newborn in your family is to hold, cuddle, love, and be a source of entertainment. Look at this age as your one chance to rock a baby in your arms while you sing songs to a captive audience! No toys required!

So sing silly songs, serious songs and everything in between. Don't be shy. No one is really listening or will remember how off-key you might be. Sing to your grandbaby with jubilation and gusto.

If you don't remember the songs from your children's baby years, here's a list to spark your memory. And if you can't remember the words, Google or YouTube them.

If You're Happy and You Know It
Head, Shoulders, Knees and Toes
Old MacDonald Had a Farm
BINGO
She'll Be Coming 'Round the Mountain
The Farmer in The Dell
Hush Little Baby
Itsy Bitsy Spider
Ten Little Monkeys
The Wheels on the Bus
The Old Gray Mare
Where is Thumbkin?
Baa Baa Black Sheep
The More We Get Together
On Top of Spaghetti
Nick Nack Paddy Whack
You Are My Sunshine

Somewhere Over the Rainbow

And don't forget to include the delightful ditty, *Baby Shark!*

There are a lot of songs not listed; this is a small list of course. Any song that rhymes or tells a story, or brings you joy to sing will work. Our personal favorite, one that became a big hit in our household, was *Yellow Submarine*.

You could add other nontraditional baby songs to your repertoire, such as songs from Elton John (*Your Song*), or Elvis (*Can't Help Falling in Love*), Nat King Cole (*L O V E*), Peter, Paul and Mary (*Michael Row the Boat Ashore*), The Andrews Sisters, (*Don't Sit Under the Apple Tree*) or additional Beatle songs (*Blackbird, Hello-Goodbye, Rocky Raccoon, I Want to Hold Your Hand, Here Comes the Sun*).

There is a lot of joy in singing to babies, for both the baby and the singer. Using silly voices or expressions as you sing can make baby laugh. And the repetition of the words gives baby a head start in expanding their vocabulary.

And speaking of vocabulary, if you want to start the communication process as early as possible, consider learning a few words in sign language. It's not hard, and there are videos you can buy, but for our needs you can find the basics of sign language for baby on YouTube. It's amazing how much infants KNOW without having the ability to verbalize. Signing to a baby as you speak or sing to them, with such simple and easy to learn signs like more, all done, up, down, sleep, hungry, eat, drink, mommy, daddy, cat and dog, gives infants a way to interact and get a jump start on connecting neural pathways for communication and comprehension.

And then there's reading. What a gratifying and fun way to broaden their horizons. While it may seem pointless to involve someone who doesn't walk, talk, or comprehend yet what you are saying to them, reading is the gateway to so many things.

According to KidsHealth.org, reading aloud to a baby offers immeasurable benefits for baby's brain.

Your voice, your closeness and the gift of reading all connect you to your grandchild in ways you may not have considered. The more stories you read to them, the more words your baby will be exposed to.

By baby's first birthday, they will learn all the sounds needed to speak their native language. If English is not your first language, don't hesitate to read to them in your native tongue. That provides an extra amount of exposure to the sounds that help build the abundant network of words that gives them a head start in vocabulary.

KidsHealth.org also states that babies who hear a lot of words, through talking or reading, frequently know more words by age two than children who have not been read to.

Reading also affects children's development in other ways as well. It helps them with their social development and thinking skills because as you hold a baby in your lap, they are encouraged to point and touch. They begin to copy sounds. They start to recognize pictures.

All of this contributes to them learning words. And it happens because you sit down to cuddle a baby as you read them a story.

Babies up to four months old are passive learners. They are most likely not showing much interest. Don't let that stop you from reading to them. Like the little sponges that they are, they are still learning, whether or not we can see it.

Four to six months old babies begin to interact with you. They will grab books, although it's usually so that they can chew on them. That's okay. There are many vinyl or cloth books with bright, vibrant colors and repetitive and/or rhyming text available.

Six to 12 months is when the magic begins! At this age your grandchild will show an interest in certain pictures because they are beginning to realize that the pictures in the books represent objects. They will indicate to you, in their own little baby way, that certain books, words, phrases or pictures have piqued their interest. Using expressive sounds and emotion in your voice adds to baby's pleasure. The magic happens when you snuggle with your little one to read a book out loud.

So don't despair that it's hard to find a variety of activities to do with infants. By reading and singing to them while you embrace them, you are creating a grandparent/grandchild connection and are making them feel safe. What a fabulous start to their new lives.

Chapter Two

Toddler and Preschool Age

What an interesting, fun, and yes, exhausting age group this is. Hopefully your grandchild takes naps, so that you will have a chance to rest and reset, but for the most part it's go, go, go!

So what can you do or play with a child this age to keep them amused? Here's a list of suggestions to get you started.

1. Hide and Seek
A timeless classic that can be played indoors or out. Take turns hiding and seeking, and let the giggles begin.

2. Board games
Board games are a fantastic way to interact with a child. But are there any board games appropriate for a very young child? Yes! There are quite a few for children who are as young as two. By playing board games you'll be giving your grandchild a heads up on the concepts of winning and losing and taking turns, in addition to allowing them to develop their psychomotor skills when it comes to things like spatial awareness and hand-eye coordination.

Games for older preschoolers are readily available with a quick Google search. Though finding the ones that work for toddlers is a little tougher, this following list of board games from *Raisecuriouskids.com* is geared specifically for two-year-olds.

Acorn Soup
Animal Upon Animal, Jr
Button, Button, Belly Button
First Orchard
Goodnight, Goodnight Construction Site Matching Game
Here Fishy, Fishy
Hungry as a Bear
Monkey Around
Nibble Munch Crunch
Panda's Picnic in the Park
Roll and Play
Topper Takes a Trip

3. Puzzles

Like board games, most puzzles are geared for older children. But there are many wooden puzzles with knobs on the pieces, which are perfect for little fingers to grasp. There are also several jigsaw puzzles on the market with only two to four large pieces, which also help with the motor skills and hand-eye coordination. The Melissa and Doug brand has a number of puzzles suitable for this age and for a variety of interests, such as safari or farm animals, vehicles, a day at the fair, underwater sea, alphabet and numbers, things around the house, etc. Plus, many of the puzzles make noise when the puzzle piece is put in the correct spot. That's instant gratification for your little one.

4. Building with blocks

There are different shapes and sizes depending on what your grandchildren enjoy. Try a variety of blocks and see which appeals to them. Legos work well with older preschoolers because they are able to manipulate those little teeny pieces well. Younger children are usually drawn to wooden blocks or over-sized cardboard blocks in a brick pattern. There are also over-sized Lego blocks which are inexpensive. Building a castle, a house for a favorite teddy bear or a doll, or a mini city awakens your grandchild's imagination.

5. Obstacle Course

Make an obstacle course in your yard or in an open space in your house. This is a simple and fun way to burn off an abundance of energy that most youngsters have.

Examples of what you can do for toddlers include:

- Place an object on the ground for them to run around in a circle.

- Lay a rope or a hula hoop on the ground for them to jump over or into.

- Set up two chairs facing one another and place a broomstick on the lowest available space for them to crawl under or step over.

– If you have a couple of bean bag chairs or large stuffed animals, you can set them up for the kids to climb over, as well. If you don't have these items, grab a bunch of pillows and put them in a huge pile. Whatever works for you.

– If you have a wooden board, encourage them to walk on it from end-to-end. A large piece of cardboard from a box works too.

Preschoolers are able to do more. You can ask them to jump in place, walk on tiptoes, stand on one foot then the other, or catch a large ball.

The last part of either obstacle course could be having them sprint to something...like your open arms!

6. Dance Contest

If you don't have enough room for an obstacle course, surely you have enough room to hold a dance contest! Hand out small prizes for the silliest dancer, the most creative dancer, or the slowest or fastest dancer. Believe me, you'll want to film this one.

7. Find the Hidden Treasure

Create a scavenger hunt to search for a hidden treasure. Place picture clues on notepaper to lead your grandchildren from one spot to another around the house or yard until they find the hidden treasure. This encourages problem solving and team work.

8. Simon Says

This game has been around for centuries. One person gives commands, and the others must follow, but only if the command starts with *Simon says*. *Simon says* put your hands in the air. *Simon says* stand on one foot. *Simon says* tap your belly. Jump up and down. You're out! Because the last command didn't include the all-important *Simon Says*! This game is a fun way to encourage listening skills.

9. Nature Exploration

Take a nature walk. Let your child gather leaves, rocks, twigs, flowers, or anything that catches their attention. Fresh air and a long, slow walk with a child. What could be better?

10. Music Parade

You can get simple musical instruments at the dollar store or tag sales almost any time. Tambourines, harmonicas, small drums, maracas, and bells are a few of the items that children love to use to make noise! If you don't have any instruments, a simple pot and a wooden spoon makes a great drum. Two paper plates glued together with uncooked rice or an old oatmeal box filled with uncooked pasta works well also. Two metal lid pots can become cymbals. Turn up the music and stage a parade around the house.

11. Cooking and baking

Small children can assist in preparing a fruit salad. You cut up the items that need a knife (apples or bananas) and let your child put in the grapes, or clementines or oranges that you've already peeled. Add either canned peaches or canned pineapple chunks without draining the syrup to stop the apples from darkening. The youngsters can pour the contents from the can and mix it together with a big spoon in a bowl. If you prefer to bake, rather than cook, allow them to add the ingredients after you've measured and again, let them stir it and help you put the batter in the pan. In this warm and loving atmosphere, they'll experience a sense of accomplishment. That's how memories are made.

12. Storytelling

Inspire their imagination by taking turns telling a story. You start with a sentence and each child adds the next sentence, taking turns. This is a collaborative activity that can lead to silliness and giggles.

13. Interactive Storytelling

Unlike the previous storytelling suggestion, you take the lead by telling or reading a story, and if you are able to, provide props and visual aids. Bring the story to life with puppets or stuffed animals. Make animal sounds or mimic the rustling of leaves or create a thunderclap with your hands. Encourage role-playing by asking your grandchildren to act out parts of the story. They can take turns being the hero, the villain or any other character. This allows them to explore different perspectives and develop their own storytelling skills. If you can provide makeshift costumes or props, all the better. But it's not necessary. For most children being involved in the story is entertaining enough.

14. Build a fort

Gather together blankets, pillows, and small tables or chairs and let them build a fort. Once it's constructed, get inside and read stories, play games or have a picnic.

15. Create a Scrapbook or a Collage

Cut out pictures from magazines. Let the children pick and choose what appeals to them (pictures of puppies and kitties or pictures of summer activities, fancy clothes or super heroes). Help them glue the items on a poster board or a scrapbook.

16. Stuffed Animal Birthday Party

Throw a birthday party for all the stuffed animals in your grandchild's life. Cupcakes, hats, balloons, the works.

17. Have a Dress Up Tea Party

This takes a little bit of planning, but it is well worth the effort, because the desired result is a memory maker. The food doesn't have to be fancy, but the clothes do! You can make slice and bake cookies or buy a treat from the bakery. Set the table with a tablecloth or a colorful sheet. Have a box of "fancy" clothes available and let the kids dress up for the tea party. It's easy to find fun hats and sparkly costume jewelry for little girls. And you'd be surprised at how much little boys like dressing up in ties, hats, and vests.

18. Self-Portrait

Roll out plain craft paper on the floor (rolls can be bought at any craft store). Have your grandchild lie down on the paper while you outline his body. Let the child draw the facial features and hair. Or you can help him glue yarn to replicate hair. Depending on the age of the child, you might want to draw the lines for the shirt and pants before he colors them in. Voila! A life-sized self- portrait.

19. Costumes Galore

Whenever you come across a tag sale or go to a thrift shop, look for things that can be used for costumes. After Halloween sales in retail stores are great for this. Cowboy hats, vests, Batman or Ninja costumes, Spider-man costumes, chef's apron and hat, princess dresses and jewelry, firefighter hats and vests, police officer hats, pirate costumes, and ballerina tutus are just the tip of the iceberg. Whenever they visit, bring out the magic box of costumes. It will entertain them for a long time.

20. Sing-Along

The list of songs from the previous chapter are repeated here, because in the previous chapter you were singing TO your grandchild. Now they are old enough to sing along with you. So, as a reminder of the types of songs that little kids love, here is the list.

If You're Happy and You Know It
Head, Shoulders, Knees and Toes

Old MacDonald Had a Farm
BINGO
She'll Be Coming 'Round the Mountain
The Farmer in The Dell
Hush Little Baby
Itsy Bitsy Spider
Ten Little Monkeys
The Wheels on the Bus
The Old Gray Mare
Where is Thumbkin?
Baa Baa Black Sheep
The More We Get Together
On Top of Spaghetti
Nick Nack Paddy Whack
You Are My Sunshine
Somewhere Over the Rainbow
Baby Shark
Your Song
Can't Help Falling in Love
L O V E
Michael Row the Boat Ashore
Don't Sit Under the Apple Tree
Blackbird
Hello-Goodbye
Rocky Raccoon
I Want to Hold Your Hand
Here Comes the Sun

Yellow Submarine

21. Paper Butterfly

Cut out a butterfly shape on white poster board. Have your grandchild paint one side of the butterfly. Fold the butterfly in half and press down so that the painted side will color the blank side. When you open it, both sides will be exactly the same. Glue a stick down the middle on the back side and your grandchild can hold it like a magic wand to make it fly.

22. Arts and Crafts

Gather together a variety of craft supplies and keep them in a box for when the grandkids visit. Wooden rubber stamps, crayons, markers, coloring books, water colors, wrapping paper, cardboard tubes, old magazines, uncooked pasta, ribbons, poster board, stickers, yarn, and buttons are a few of the things you can use. It can get messy, but that's part of the fun. Give each child a large t-shirt, cover your table with an old sheet or a big piece of cardboard and have at it. It's a great way to nurture artistic talent.

Here are several ideas for arts and crafts you can create together with your grandchildren.

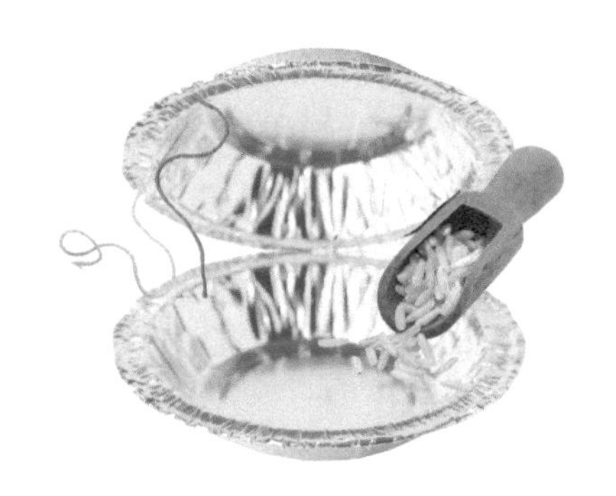

a. Tambourine

If you are a music loving family, why not make a tambourine? Take two aluminum pie plates (paper plates work too, but not as well). With a hole puncher, punch holes around each plate. Make each hole the same distance apart so that the holes in the plates line up. Put pebbles or uncooked rice into one of the plates. Cover with the other plate. Weave yarn through the holes and tie a strong knot.

b. Make a Homemade Nightshirt

We did this when our children were little and I saved them for when they had children of their own. We bought plain white men's large t-shirts and had each child paint whatever they liked on it. The only criteria we insisted upon was that somewhere on the shirt was their name, the date, and a hand print. After that they were free to create. You can imagine our son's surprise when 25 years later we gifted him his "nightshirt" with

Darkwing Duck painted on it!

c. Placemats

Take a piece of construction paper and draw a circle the size of a dinner plate in the center. Have the children decorate outside the circle by making a collage with spare photos. Or they can use stickers, wooden rubber stamps, or markers to draw whatever they want. Laminate the placemats when finished,

d. Handprint or Footprint Art

Use non-toxic paint to turn your grandchildren's handprints or footprints into animals, flowers or anything else your imagination (or theirs) can conjure up.

e. Windsock

Have your grandchild decorate one side of a piece of construction paper. You could make theme windsocks by coloring them red, white and blue for a patriotic theme or using moons and stars for a nighttime theme. Then have them cut nine 25-inch crepe paper streamers and glue them to the back on the bottom. Glue the decorated construction paper together to form a tube. On the top of the tube, punch two holes and add a piece of string for hanging.

f. Finger painting

Place a large sheet of paper on a table (outside is best, but with the right preparation inside works too). Allow them to finger paint with paint or pudding. If you want to keep mess to a minimum, put a smaller piece of paper in a throw away aluminum foil baking pan.

You can help your grandchild make a correlation between the finger painting that you do together and the art work that is displayed in art museums. Make an effort to visit one. It doesn't have to be the New York Metropolitan Museum of Art. There are many local art museums to visit whose admissions are reasonably priced or free on certain days and times. To make it fun for a child, buy three or four postcards at the gift shop and have her search the museum to find the pictures on the postcards. Ask her questions about the color, shapes or scenery. Ask her if she likes a particular painting or not. Let her use her eyes to describe the artwork to you. You may see something you hadn't noticed before.

Chapter Three

Winter and/or Christmas Crafts - Preschool to Early Elementary

Rudolph the Red Nosed Reindeer

This fun project will go smoothly if you prepare in advance. You will need two different shades of brown construction paper, a small red circle, either a pom pom or a small piece of red felt or construction paper, and two googly eyes or two white circles and two smaller black circles to make the eyes.

Trace your grandchild's shoe on a piece of brown construction paper and cut it out. Then trace each of their hands onto a lighter piece of brown construction paper. It could be traced onto darker paper as well. The idea is to show a contrast between the two browns. Have your grandchild glue the hand tracing to the heel part of the paper shoe to make antlers before they glue on the nose and eyes. Punch a hole at the top between the two antlers, add a piece of ribbon, and you have a reindeer ornament.

Santa Pops

Buy refrigerated sugar cookie dough. Slice them into 12-18 slices. On an ungreased baking sheet flatten each slice on top of a craft stick. Bake, then cool completely. Depending on what you know of your grandchild's attention span, you may want to do the baking and cooling before you are ready to do the craft.

Lightly spread white frosting on each cookie. Place two blue M&M's on the face for eyes and one red one for a nose. Sprinkle red sprinkles on top for his hat and add a mini-marshmallow on the side for a pom pom.

Marshmallow Snowmen

Attach three large marshmallows together using pretzel sticks. Insert small pieces of pretzel in the side for arms. Decorate with candies for buttons and writing gel for faces. A gumdrop makes a great hat.

Picture Ornament

Buy a package of inexpensive doilies. Have your grandchild lightly run a glue stick over one doily and place a favorite photo directly in the center. Cut out a circle in the center of a second doily and place it on top of the uncut doily, making sure the photo can be seen. Run the glue stick on the front side of the ornament, so that they can sprinkle glitter on it. Punch a hole on top, add ribbon and hang it on the tree.

Snowflakes

If you do a little prep work on this, you can make a bunch of snowflakes with minimal mess. You'll need a freezer bag, paper plates, poster paint and glitter. The poster paint can be any color, but it you are going for a realistic snowflake, you might want to stick with pale blue, white and silver.

You will need to pre-cut the snowflakes. Fold a paper plate in half and then in half again. You can do another half if you'd like, but after that it gets nearly impossible to cut. Cut some designs (half circles and triangles) and then open up the snowflake.

Have your grandchild slide the snowflake in the freezer bag and let them squirt a minimal amount of poster paint inside. Sprinkle in a bit of glitter and close the bag completely. (Make sure most of the air is removed).

Show your grandchild how to spread the colors around by laying her hands flat on the bag and smoothing it out. The more it spreads, the more decorated the snowflake will be. Carefully, take the snowflake out of the bag and leave it to dry. If you want an extra sparkly snowflake, add additional glitter before it dries.

Chapter Four

Elementary Age

Children in the early elementary years are interested in the world around them and are keen to share what they know and what they've learned. And best of all, they are at the age where *they believe what you tell them*. *They look*

to you for advice and are inclined to listen and learn. It's absolutely magical!

That's why I call the ages from six to 11 the *Wonder Years*. They can read independently, yet they still relish being read to. The chapter books that are geared for them are more engrossing than a picture book because these books are filled with imaginative plots, twists and turns, and spine-tingling chapter endings.

As grandparents, we want to take advantage of these golden years. This is the time when they are willing and able to learn new hobbies and where they genuinely love the quality time you are able to spend with them. If you like to cook or fish or camp or hike or even go to tag sales to search for ceramic rabbits for your collection, most likely they will too. If you take pleasure spending an hour in the library searching for a few good reads, so will they. If you are a mall shopper and take them with you, they'll revel in a day at the mall.

The sky's the limit during this special time in their lives. Make it matter.

Fun Places to Explore

While amusement parks are always a great place to spend a fun day with your grandchildren, they are not the only option available.

Remember the art museum for younger children? Well, it's even more fun at this age. Local art museums usually have reasonably priced or free admission on certain days and times.

To encourage your grandchild to look at art and think about it, ask them questions about what type of art appeals to them and why. Do they prefer landscapes, portraits, or sculptures? What do they see when they look at a piece of art that appeals to them?

Encourage them to use their eyes and their vision to explain how they perceive the art work.

You don't need to be a teacher. You can be the student.

Not interested in art? That's not a problem. Because in almost any city or town in the US, you'll find unique, sometimes wacky, museums nearby to explore. From the serious to the silly, a day at a museum is worth it.

A search within a 60-minute drive from our house yielded over 50 large and small ones.

The range of museums was amazing: art museums, kid's interactive museums, firefighter, local historical, railway, Veterans and military museums, American Indian Study museum, nature museums and preserves, a whaling museum, an Audubon Birdcraft museum, and a carousel museum. There was even a castle open for visitation.

We also are lucky enough to have the Mark Twain House and the Harriet Beecher Stowe house within driving distance and we have been able to visit the Webb Deane Stevens Museum where George Washington planned the Battle of York. All within 50 miles of us. So do a quick Google search.

No matter where you live, there is something to see or do nearby. Check it out. You might be surprised. I know I was.

Fall and Winter

If the weather outside is frightful, here are a handful of ideas to preoccupy the kids for the day.

1. Summer picnic

Enjoy a summer picnic in your living room. Spread a blanket or a sheet on the floor. Turn up the heat a few degrees and serve summer picnic foods, such as egg salad or tuna sandwiches, watermelon and potato chips on paper plates. If you have the room, after cleanup, toss around a beach ball or play with a foam Frisbee.

2. Flower arrangements

If the house seems dreary in the middle of the deepest darkest winter, buy an inexpensive bouquet of flowers from the supermarket. Grab a bunch of small or single bud vases, drinking glasses and/or empty spice containers, and allow each child to create their own floral arrangement to take home with them for their bedroom.

3. Board Game Marathon

Now that the children are older, board games are really a blast. Set up a few folding tables with a different board game on each. You can start at one table, play the game, then move onto the next round robin style.

4. Card games

Uno, Crazy Eights, Go Fish, and Old Maid are a few examples of card games this age group enjoys. Do you know a card trick or two? Teach it to them. If you don't know any, look up some videos on YouTube and learn a few simple ones.

5. Mini Golf course

Like the previously mentioned obstacle course, this one works well for older kids. Create a mini-golf course using household items such as cups, cardboard ramps, books and stuffed animals. Make tunnels out of the books, or cut holes in a cardboard box. Place stuffed animals to be used as obstacles. You can use a whiffle ball and a plastic bat (which can often be found at the Dollar Store), or you buy golf sets for children which cost around $10-$15.

Outdoor Fun

Get outside for a while. No matter how damp or dreary the weather is, it's good to get outside occasionally and be a kid again.

1. Make a Scarecrow

Put an old shirt and hat on top of a broomstick. Stuff him with newspapers or leaves.

2. Pretend Pumpkins

Stuff leaves into bags and decorate them like pumpkins.

3. Hill Rolling

Find a hill and watch and applaud as your grandkids roll down it over and over again.

4. Nature Walk

Take a nature walk and play "I Spy" or call it a "Walk of Color" and search for items in yellow, red, orange and brown.

5. Spooky Hide and Seek

Go outside at dusk and play Hide and Seek using glow sticks.

6. Snow Time

Don't let a little snow stop you! Make a snowman, build a fort or have a good old-fashioned snowball fight. And speaking of snowball fights, there is no reason you can't have one in the house (not with real snow of course). If you crochet, they are quick and easy to make. Or if you prefer, you can buy a fake snowball set to play with indoors.

Spring and Summer

1. Paint Party

Tape large sheets of white paper or poster board to the outside wall of the house using masking tape. Give each child a smock, or a man's large t-shirt to wear and have them paint a picture. You can frame them by putting decorative masking tape (washi tape) around the edges.

2. Science Experiment

To make a volcano, you don't need to buy a fancy kit. Find a tall glass or a wide mouth vase and put in a cup of baking soda. Permit your grandchild to slowly pour vinegar in the cup and watch the volcano erupt. It gets messy, so either do it in the sink or on a tray.

3. Mini Science Lesson

Take a few sheets of dark colored construction paper outside and place it in direct sunlight. Have the children decorate the sheets with a variety of leaves. Each leaf should have its own space, so they don't overlap. Wait a few hours and then remove the leaves; their patterned outlines will remain.

4. Picnic Prep

If you're planning on taking the kids to the park, why not make it a full-blown picnic? Instead of only packing snacks, have them help you make egg salad or tuna sandwiches and a salad.

5. Instant Greenhouse

Plant seeds or a tiny plant inside a small container; a cottage cheese container works well. Cut off the top of a soda bottle and discard. Place the remaining part of the bottle upside down over the plant and you have an instant greenhouse. Each time the child comes to visit, measure the plant and mark down the progress and date on an index card.

6. Lava Lamp

You'll need a clean jar or a tall glass, vegetable oil, water, food coloring and an antacid tablet, like Alka-Seltzer. Fill the jar about half way with vegetable oil, then add water until the jar is at least ¾ full, but don't fill all the way to the top. Add 10 drops of food coloring. Break the antacid tablet into small pieces. Drop the pieces into the jar one at a time. Watch your lava lamp activate!

7. Reading Tree

Make a reading tree by drawing a huge five-foot tree with bare branches on a large sheet of white paper (rolls of white paper can be found at your local craft store). Draw construction paper leaf patterns. Have the children trace and cut several leaves. Use the tree as a reading tree with each leaf representing a different book that's been read. Write the name of the child, the book title and the author on each leaf as a child completes a book and tape it to the tree. The goal is to see how long it takes to fill the tree up with leaves.

8. Sock Puppets

Who doesn't love sock puppets? This never gets old for most kids. Give them your lonely, unattached socks along with buttons, yarn and glue and let them create a sock puppet family.

9. Stargazing

Plan a nighttime picnic and stargazing expedition. Gather blankets and munchies and go outside for a nighttime picnic. The best time to do this is around August 12th when the Perseid meteor shower appears. With luck, you may see some shooting stars. You don't have to be a first-class astronomer to teach them a few things about the night sky. Almost anyone can find the Big Dipper. It's also easy to spot a few planets. These are the "stars that don't twinkle." The brightest one is Venus, the reddish one is Mars. Snuggle under the blankets and savor the special memories you are making.

10. Relay Race

Have a relay race where players must balance a golf ball or a hardboiled egg on a spoon and race by walking quickly from one point to another without dropping the egg.

11. Pin the tail on the Monkey

Draw a monkey, a donkey, or any other animal on a piece of poster board and make several numbered tails with a piece of double-sided tape on the top of each tail. Taking turns, wrap a scarf around the child's eyes and have them try to pin the tail on the monkey while they are blindfolded.

12. Books Galore

Never let your grandchild go home without a gift book from you. We collect them from thrift shops and tag sales and have a big box always at the ready. When it's time for Mom or Dad to pick up the kids, have the children pick a book from the box. A little tip for you on this one. Rotate the books that you have in your book box. And limit the number of books to where each child will only have four or five choices. If there are too many choices, children can get overwhelmed. They worry that they'll pick the "wrong" book and will change their minds seven or eight times before they actually get out the door.

Ask me how I know this!

Chapter Five

Preteens and Teens

Preteens and teenagers are remarkable people. They are less than a decade away from being on their own and there is a lot for them to absorb and figure out in their last stretch to adulthood. As grandparents, we want to be able to influence them without preaching and give them a helping hand into this final journey before they are off on their own.

Kids this age are going through a lot of changes. Their bodies are changing almost daily, as are many of their relationships with their peers.

But one thing never changes. It has always been, as it was when we were young, that as a rule, teens spend more time with each other and less time with adults.

However, the thing that has changed is the added mix of technology and screen time kids are exposed to. There's a tremendous amount of pressure on teens today because of social media. They have to deal with stuff that we never had to think about. For example, remember when you did something embarrassing in middle or high school? You were teased and laughed at and you were humiliated and mortified...for weeks! And then someone else did something embarrassing and your situation was forgotten. It would fade away into the subconscious of everyone's mind.

But today, if a kid does something embarrassing, it might be caught on video, and then turned into a meme and put on Snapchat or Tik Tok. And everybody in the entire school sees it. And someone takes a screen shot of it. And it gets spread further. And the kid can't get away from it, because no one forgets and they are still sharing it months later.

Remember how hard it was to deal with the humiliation for a few weeks? What if you had to deal with it the entire time you were in high school?

You can help with your grandchildren's transition into adulthood by being the grandparent they want to spend time with. You don't want to be the curmudgeon who doesn't understand or appreciate the difficulties that face preteens and teens today. And you certainly don't want to be a dividing wedge between the two generations.

It's a two-way street. You can't expect to have your grandchild sit and listen to you drone on about the "good old days" without taking the same amount of time to listen to them describe the adversities that they face today.

In order to be that bridge between the generations, we, the grandparents, have to be the ones to take the first step. It starts with us.

The first thing that you have to do is to accept the fact that no matter what you do, your grandchildren are going to become teenagers. That burst of happiness you got when they were little and would scream, "Nana!" (Or Grandma or Mimi or Poppa or Grampy or whatever) and would throw themselves into your arms is gone.

But take heart. It's the way it is supposed to be. Friends

increasingly become the center of their world. If all you get is a simple nod or a perfunctory hug, accept it for what it is. Your grandchildren are growing up and are slowly distancing themselves from the people they love. Mom and Dad feel it. So will you. But that doesn't mean they don't need you, or want to be with you. It just has to be on their terms. If you can hang in there long enough, they might discover that you are what they need right now. At this stage it's not about the amount of time you spend with your grandchild, rather it's about the amount of attention you can give them at this most confusing stage of their young lives.

Of course, it helps if you live close enough to visit whenever you want. This is not always possible. Geographic distance can be a burden. If you are unhealthy, unfit, or financially unable to be close geographically, it does add an extra obstacle.

But that's where the technology that I mentioned earlier comes into play. FaceTime, Skype, Microsoft Teams or other video chat platforms can be such a game changer. A weekly five-minute call can keep the lines of communication open.

And don't forget texting. Older grandchildren love to text. Sending a text here and there to wish them well on a school project or test, or to encourage them on a day that you know might be a tough one, speaks volumes. Don't blow up their phones with texts. A quick line or two to encourage and lift the spirits of your grandchild is what they will appreciate most.

Be grateful for the social networking sites that can keep you in touch with tweens, teens and young adult grandchildren. Stay positive and uncritical; researchers say a gap between the generations develops when the younger generation finds us senior citizens to be hypocritical and/or lacking in social tolerance. The absolute most important factor for ensuring a closeness with your grandchild rests on the attitude of the grandparent. We are the ones who need to put in the effort. It boils down to this: It is the grandparent who is determined to build a strong and enduring relationship with their grandchildren who is the one most likely to succeed.

So what can you do?

I did a lot of research to answer that question. I listened to the advice of several professional experts and then I went and surveyed experts that did not have a degree or any letters after their name. I asked those in the trenches...the grandparents who have a particularly good relationship with their teen and young adult grandchildren.

I asked them what it was that they did to ensure a long-lasting relationship with their descendants.

This is what they told me.

1. Make spending time with your grandchild a priority

Remember how fast their baby, toddler, preschool years flew by? How about elementary school? One day they were in kindergarten and in what seems like 15 minutes, they were heading into middle school.

Well, the teen years don't go any slower. In fact, they speed up!

Don't put off visits to them when you can make it. Are they in a sport? Are they in choir or the theater group? Go to see every event humanly possible. They will truly appreciate it even if they don't say so. I can guarantee that because the world evolves around them at this stage (and admit it, it was true for us when we were teenagers as well), they might not understand how special it is that you do this for them. But when they get older and out into the world, they will learn from friends that not everyone had the same type of grandparents that they did. And they will look back on your commitment years later and be deeply grateful for having had you in their lives.

2. Respect their boundaries when it comes to social media

Think back on your teenage years. If you'd had social media, would you have wanted your parents or your grandparents to see whatever you posted? Of course not! So don't take it personally or be offended if they don't want to include you in their "friend" group. There are other ways to connect through technology. And while we're on the subject of technology...

3. Be the student occasionally

Ask for their help and advice when it comes to the latest social media trend.

No matter how well informed you are as far as social media and electronic devices go, you can be relatively sure they know more. They will know all about the latest apps, etc.

Tell them what your interests are and they'll be able to help you find an app that will broaden your knowledge on the subject. Ask them how they would like you to stay connected with them. It could be Zoom, Skype, FaceTime, texts, What's app, or something else that hasn't been created yet. Most teens would love to be the teacher to help you learn about their world as it is today.

4. Make them number one, not you!

Focus on *their* interests, *their* activities, *their* social, school and home lives. You had your turn when you were a teen. Pass the baton and make it all about them. Show them with your actions that you are interested in them as people and not simply because they are your grandchildren. Do they love painting? Pets? Theater? Movies? Music? Dance? Do they belong to the chess club, the debate team, the cheerleading squad or the basketball team? Express an interest in whatever subject they love. You will be building a bridge and you might discover to your surprise that you actually like football or swim meets or whatever it is they are doing that you thought you could never be entertained by.

5. Listen to them without judgment

Let them know you love them as much now as you did when they were precious little toddlers. These years are hard on them and they are under enormous pressure. They feel scrutiny and judgment from all angles: their peers, their teachers, maybe their parents, basically from society in general. They're trying to figure it all out with a lot of conflicting information, pressure and influences from all sides. Be the good influence. Stay silent and allow them to talk. Sometimes all you need to do is listen.

Now that you know the best way to keep the communication open, what types of things can you do to encourage it?

6. Take a car ride with your teen alone

This was one of the best pieces of advice I got when my sons were heading into their teen years. A wise woman said to me, "People always think that if you want to get teens to open up, that you should schedule some alone time with them and offer them a cup of hot chocolate or tea and sit down at the kitchen table together for a one-on-one. The problem is, it doesn't turn out the way you picture it in your head.

"First of all, there are potential interruptions. The phone rings, the dog barks, your spouse comes into the kitchen to get a snack. And worst of all, at least in the eyes of your teen, you are looking at them face-to-face."

Her advice was as follows (and I can attest to it that it

truly worked for us). “Turn off your phone and take your teen with you to do errands or to pick up the pizza.”

You will be surprised on how much they will open up if they are confident that they won’t be interrupted by outside forces. They'll feel comfortable because they don’t have to face you eye-to-eye. With both of you in close proximity, yet not looking at each other, often the floodgates open up.

Whether or not they are willing to discuss a problem they are having with school or friends or they tell you about the new kid in class that they like, you will be amazed at what they will share if there is no pressure and no distractions.

And one other thing to keep in mind. Many adults don’t talk to teens as though they are equals. It can mean so much to older kids if you include them in discussions that pertain to them and their lives. Often, they are treated as though they are invisible and not the productive citizens we expect them to be in a few short years. So ask for their advice on how to fix things or ask them their opinion on current events. Doing so can give you a deeper connection and it will go a long way to make both generations feeling respected.

7. Be their cheerleader

They've got parents and teachers and coaches who are constantly guiding them to be the best they can be whether it's on the softball team, grasping tough math equations, or striving to become a future good citizen. They don't need another person telling them what to do. They need someone in their corner as a cheerleader who accepts them with all of their teenage angst and mistakes. Let them know you love them no matter how they look or how well they are doing in school, or whatever youthful mistakes they've made. We all were young once and many of us made doozies of mistakes.

Be their cheerleader and they will remember it forever.

So what can you actually do with teens to create a bond?

Here are a few suggestions:

1. Learn how to play video games

Think you'll never be able to master the controller? You will. It's like every other skill you've acquired. All you need is practice.

2. Read whatever books they are assigned in school in tandem with them

Find out what book they are assigned to read in school and read along with them. Reading *Moby Dick* might have been tough when you were young, but it's a remarkable book when you are older. So, if they need to read Chapters 1-3 of *Moby Dick* by Friday, read chapters 1-3 and text or call them to discuss it. Let them complain about how challenging it is, then bring the conversation back to what you found to be the most poignant or interesting parts. Ask them questions about the chapters. Your take on the book can open their eyes in ways they hadn't thought of before.

3. Teach a Skill

Do you have a skill? Of course you do! Do you play the piano, the cello or the guitar? How about the harmonica? Do you sew, crochet or knit? Do you paint or draw?

Do you know your way around cars? Are you a great cook or a fabulous baker? Are you good with money management? Can you fix a leaky faucet?

Do you have a garden that you love to work in? Can you play chess? Are you a good writer?

Whenever a grandchild shows an interest in anything that you know and could share, offer to teach it to them. On some of your skill sets, you don't actually need to offer to teach. Do you plan on working under the hood of your car? Wait until they come to visit for a day and ask them for their help. The same holds true for things like gardening or fixing a leaky faucet. You'll get a helper, they'll learn a life skill, and you'll have the added bonus of being able to have a pleasant conversation without any distractions.

4. Create a traditions wish list

Provide each grandchild with a sheet of paper and ask them to write down their ideas for possible new traditions. You might not be able to do them all, but you also might be surprised to see what they come up with. Since each child is an individual with individual tastes, try to do a separate tradition with each child, even if it means taking turns when they visit. For example, if one child loves to collect rocks, go on a rock hunting excursion with just that child, if possible. Divide and conquer if you can. You go on a walk to collect rocks, while Grandpa spends the day with the others doing Grandpa things. Rotate each time they come so that every child has special alone time with a grandparent.

Things to do when you are together, besides the aforementioned video games.

Culinary Ideas

1. Create your own pizza night

Buy pre-made dough or make it from scratch if you're feeling really ambitious. Provide a variety of toppings, so that each child can indulge in making their own creation.

2. Pancakes for dinner (or lunch or breakfast)

Make a batch of pancakes and teach the children how to flip them. Provide cut-up fresh fruit, whipped cream, and a variety of syrups.

3. International Cuisine Day

Pick a country and prepare a meal together from that country's cuisine. Play the traditional music from the area as you cook. If you're really enthusiastic about it, you can make a flag from the country on poster board before the kids arrive or they can make it while the meal cooks. Also, while the meal is cooking, look up interesting/fun facts about the culture. You might be surprised at how much all of you learn.

4. Farmer's Market Adventure

Nothing tastes better than fruit or vegetables that are stunningly fresh. If you have a local farmer's market nearby, visit it with your grandchildren.

Community Involvement

Are you the type of person who gives back to your community? If yes, why not include your grandchildren in your quest to make the world a better place?

Here are a few ideas to get you started.

1. Volunteer Together

Find local volunteer opportunities that are geared toward your grandchildren's interests. It can be as involved as you like. You can help at a food bank or participate in a park cleanup. If that requires more time than you can spare on their visit, consider taking the children shopping for dog or cat food and supplies and have the children drop the supplies off at your local animal shelter.

2. Bake and Share

Bake homemade goods and deliver them to a struggling neighbor or a nursing home. The police and fire department also appreciate the thoughtfulness of receiving home-baked goods.

3. Create Care Packages

Assemble care packages with essential items and treats and distribute them to the homeless in your area. Or find an organization that is in need and gather items from their most requested list and drop it off to the organization.

4. Visit a Nursing Home

Call a nursing home in your area and find out when is a good time to visit its residents. There are many lonely elderly people who would appreciate a visit from some young people who could provide companionship. Bring a variety of flowers to brighten their day. Or ask your grandchild to paint a few pictures to bring along as gifts.

5. Participate in a Charity Run/Walk

Are you a runner? Sign up for charity walks or runs together. The physical activity is a bonus. The real gift is supporting causes you care about with someone you love and who shares your passion.

6. Make Homemade Greeting Cards

Children's hospitals, nursing homes, and our troops overseas love to receive greeting cards from random strangers. If your grandchild is creative and loves to draw or color, this is a perfect opportunity to get them involved. It doesn't really matter if the artwork is great or mediocre. In this case it truly is the thought that counts.

7. Random Acts of Kindness Day

Dedicate a day to performing random act of kindness. You could offer to pay for a patron's donuts or drink at your local coffee shop. Why not buy a bunch of flowers and have your grandchild hand out one to each person they meet on your walk? Maybe your grandchild would like to write a few positive, encouraging notes to tuck away in random places in town. These are things that take little or no effort and yet give back a huge reward in the feel-good department of our lives.

Crafts to Do with Your Teen or Preteen

1. Collage Creations

This activity is great for encouraging dialog, as you are sitting at a table together working on a project, yet not looking directly at one another. It relaxes most kids, even as it sparks their artistic juices.

Gather old magazines and/or newspapers and create collages. It can be centered on a specific theme or you can go in the other direction and do a free-for-all.

2. Nature Inspired Art

Take a nature walk with your grandchild and collect leaves, twigs, and rocks. Use these materials to create a nature themed display. You can do an artistic exhibit freestyle on a coffee table or sideboard or you can display your treasures in a large bowl to adorn your dining room or bedside table.

3. Mosaic Art

Use small pieces of colored glass, tiles, small beans or pasta, tiny seashells, broken pottery, or whatever you can conjure up to create mosaic art. You can make a mosaic picture frame, or go large and make a tabletop or stepping stones for the garden.

4. Comic Book Creation

Buy a blank comic book to collaborate on. Plan out the plot and characters before you start doing the actual drawing. (Writers call it a rough draft, children call it a sloppy copy). Once you have it designed and ready to go, fill out the panels together. If you have a few grandchildren in this age group I suggest you have a separate book for each child.

5. Tie-Dye T-shirts

Everything old is new again! Have a tie-dye party where you and your grandchildren design colorful custom shirts. It's a fun, messy project that yields unique results. Prep the fabric by prewashing it before the grandkids come over. To make a tie-dye t-shirt, secure different sections with rubber bands. Add dye color on each sectioned off area.

Now comes the hard part. Let your project set for at least 6 hours, but optimally overnight. Remove the rubber bands to reveal the design. Wash, dry, then wear!

Chapter Six

Long Distance Grandparenting

Almost every grandparent fantasizes about what life will be like when grandchildren come into the picture.

But occasionally life throws you a curve, and for whatever reason, your children don't live near enough for you to see your grandchildren on a regular basis.

It can be heart-wrenching when you are surrounded by friends who live near their own grandchildren and who post photos on social media of their grandkids at family birthday parties, baseball games or amusement parks.

It can become difficult to be around those friends who are able to bask in the joys and delights of their new family and who, of course, like to talk about it.

As painful as that may be for you, there are many older adults who, for a variety of reasons, never get to be a grandparent at all. Your position is an enviable one for them, because you are blessed to have grandchildren with whom you can get close to emotionally even if distance separates you physically.

For those who find themselves long-distance grandparents, you are not alone. In fact, according to AARP's 2019 Grandparents Today study, over half of grandparents in the US have at least one grandchild who lives at least 200 miles away.

That's the bad news.

The good news is we are not living in the pioneer era when people set out to go west and left family behind. Mail service was erratic at best. Photographs were virtually nonexistent and technology was over a hundred years away. Once a family moved, the chance at any relationship at all with the grandchildren vanished.

But not today. We have a plethora of ways to stay connected with our families, no matter how many states or oceans divide us.

You, as the loving grandparent, are the one who needs to bridge the distance between the two generations if you can't be there in person. It takes some planning and extra effort on your part, but the trade-off is worth it.

Here are some suggestions which I hope will help you in your quest to be as devoted to your grandchildren as possible.

For All Ages

1. Skype, FaceTime, Google Duo or any other similar services

Phone calls are fun, but seeing your grandkids, and having them see you, is better. No, it's not the same as having them in the room with you where you can give them a hug and a squeeze. But being able to see each other in our personal surroundings makes us feel closer than hearing a solitary voice on the phone. These types of calls work best if they are set up in advance as a weekly date. That way you can be sure to find a time that is convenient for all.

The attention span of little ones is minimal, at best. While they love watching you and listening to you as you read books to them, recognize that they might not make it through the whole book. After all, they can't hug or touch you either, so you have no more credence than a character on a TV or computer screen. Don't be surprised if they lose interest within a nanosecond. If that's the case, go with the flow. Don't take it personally.

Invite them to show you their room or their toys. Ask them questions about their environment. Our own personal experience taught us that when our grandchildren were really young and had the attention span of a gnat, their mom or dad would set the phone on the couch and the children would play in front of it because the grandkids wanted an audience.

No, it was not stimulating conversation and yes, sometimes it seemed like we'd be captive audiences forever. It was often time-consuming and our dinners got cold repeatedly waiting for them to finish a never-ending diatribe on nothing. But you know what? It paid off big time in the long run. Now we have genuine conversations about actual subjects.

This metamorphosis occurred because we paid attention to them when they were cute and sweet, even though the dialog was unintelligible and monotonous beyond belief.

Keep at it and you'll note that slowly, week after week, they'll establish a stronger connection with you and will stay online longer and with more enthusiasm. At that point you can teach them a new song each week or play games with them in real time.

Truly, it's the next best thing to being there.

And here's an extra thought. Have a list of questions or prompts available for when they call and there is a lull in the conversation.

Ask them what they did in their preschool class or what made them laugh today. Ask them to describe their favorite shirt or toy. Have them tell you what they had for dinner and what their favorite snack is in the whole world. This will keep little ones engaged a while longer and make the time on the phone with them much more riveting than watching them run back and forth in front of the phone camera.

And definitely keep a cheat sheet handy when talking to older kids. Make a list of the names of their friends, their teachers, their pets, and the classes that they take. It will encourage a deeper conversation if you can say, *Are you and Melissa hanging out this weekend?* rather than *So do you have any plans with any of your friends?*

Also, for older kids, an occasional spontaneous call is appreciated if you are calling to wish a child good luck on a spelling test or a basketball game. Keep those calls short and sweet, however. You remember how busy your schedule was when you were young. A quick *hello* and *I'm thinking of you* goes a long way.

2. Snail Mail is Always a Winner

Everyone loves getting mail.

Most of us are at the age where we remember how fabulous it felt to get a letter or card in the mail. It still gives me a thrill! Our grandchildren are rarely, if ever, going to get letters the way we did when we were young. Everything is done with technology today.

But you can still give your grandchildren that anticipatory thrill by sending them something every once in a while. Send toddlers, preschoolers, and early elementary age kids a card and add a coloring book page or a connect-the-dots or find-a-word page every week.

In fact, why not create a word search specifically with your grandchild in mind?

Design a word search where he or she has to find their name (first, middle and last) scattered throughout the puzzle. Also include things they love, such as their favorite teddy bear's name or their favorite color. This is simple to do and it is so personalized that most kids love it.

Or, if you prefer, on occasion, send them a small package with a soft covered book, a coloring book or stickers. Get creative! If you crochet, make a little heart or butterfly. If you don't, search for tiny objects in the dollar store that fit in a small envelope. Extravagant gifts aren't required. A little key chain, a postcard, a bookmark, a mini notepad, or a photo of something that kids love is all that's needed.

And don't forget older elementary age grandchildren. Do your grandkids collect Pokemon cards or baseball/football cards? Send a small package with cards or a book to make their day.

You might think that it's harder to find things to send to teens, but with a little contemplation you can make their day too. It's not that difficult to find a fun note card where you can add a word of encouragement or a funny joke you think they'd appreciate.

You could include a $10 gift card to Subway, McDonalds, or Starbucks from time-to-time for an unexpected surprise. Snail mail is an easy way to stay involved.

A note of warning...please be aware that most school districts do not teach cursive anymore. So children can't read "fancy" writing as my young grandson calls it. Whether that's a good thing or not, it is a fact. For example, we had written letters to our grandchildren on their first birthday to be opened when they turn 18. We have since had to rewrite them because we are not sure if they will be able to read them in cursive. Our reasoning for writing the letters in cursive in the first place was because we thought it would feel special and be more personal. So, if you are going to go the mail route, be sure each letter, card or note is either printed or typewritten.

3. Become a Pen Pal

Since we've already established that everyone loves mail, why not take it a step further and become pen pals with your grandkids? For very young children, send them a note along with a self-addressed stamped envelope and ask them to draw a picture for you. (To be honest, a self-addressed stamped envelope would be a good idea for all ages. Can you imagine a teen looking for an envelope, a stamp and your address? If you are hoping to make this work, supply a self-addressed return envelope).

Kids who are learning to print get excited with the idea of becoming a pen pal. It helps to build their confidence when they grasp the concept that they are able to write a real letter. Don't expect too much. Ask them a question in your letter that they can answer in a sentence or two. The idea is to encourage their enthusiasm and ignite the spark and the joy of getting and receiving mail.

And for more experienced writers, the kids who are old enough to decode a message, take the time to write to them using a secret code. You can use numbers to replace the letters of the alphabet or you can establish your own special code that is shared between you and your grandchild. An example might be substituting shapes for letters, such as star=A, circle=B, square=C, etc. To make it even more thrilling for them, write *Top Secret* or *Confidential* on the outside of the envelope.

Another project is to write an ongoing story together. You write seven words to open the story and mail it to your grandchild. Have your grandchild write an additional seven words to keep the story going to send back to you. Create a different story for each grandchild. Who knows? You may develop an up-and-coming author with this technique.

Is your grandchild a budding artist? You can do the same thing with a picture. Draw something on a piece of paper and send it to them to add to the drawing. You can have a prearranged limit on the number of objects to be drawn on the picture each time you mail it back and forth.

For example, you draw an outline of a house with no

windows, doors, chimney, etc. Maybe you add a fence and a tree. Send it to them and ask them to draw three items on the page. If they don't fill in the house with its doors and windows, then you can add those next time on your turn. Keep it going until you have a masterpiece, suitable for hanging.

If your grandkids aren't teens yet, now is the time to start the writing back and forth to one another. If you don't start writing to them from the time they are little, you can't expect to get a huge result when they are older. Be grateful for whatever communication you can get from a teen.

However, if you are lucky enough to have a teen who would enjoy being a pen pal with you, be considerate of their hectic schedule. They don't have the time or energy to write a three-page letter.

But, if you have already established a writing relationship with your teen grandchild, why not send an occasional photo of yourself when you were their age?

Did you go to prom? Send them a copy of your prom photo. Did you play a sport? Send a photo. How about sending a picture of your first car when they learn to drive? They might not respond to all of your gestures the way you hope they do, but they are still developing a relationship with you.

And that is the goal; to establish an ongoing relationship.

So, we have to be the ones who put in the effort if we want to see results.

4. Watch a TV show together

Pick a show and watch it either at the same time, where you can chat about it while it's happening, or watch it separately and discuss it later at an agreed upon time. Let them choose the show. Some of what they want to watch might not interest you, especially if your grandchild is really young. Do it anyway! You may end up being surprised because a lot of kid shows (think about shows like Rocky and Bullwinkle) have jokes that are secretly geared towards adults.

It builds a bridge of communication and shows your grandchild, no matter what their age, that you take them and their interests seriously.

5. Share their interests with a mutual magazine subscription

Get a magazine subscription for a grandchild and get one for yourself as well. Although these can be done online, getting a physical copy of the magazine is always exciting. After you both receive your copy read the articles and discuss them via FaceTime or Skype. There are magazines available for any interest your grandchild may have.

6. Play board games

You can play a board game with your grandchild and not be in the same room! Isn't technology spectacular? For preschoolers, who don't understand how to follow the rules yet, the physical game should be at their house. They roll the dice, pick the cards or whatever is needed to play the game. They take turns and move the pieces for both of you.

For older kids, it's really fun if you both have the same game and can play it together. Each person moves the pieces for both parties, so the boards will be (or should be) identical. Games like this are almost as fun as being there.

For Little Ones to Preteens

1. Record bedtime stories on video

Record yourself reading several books. We did this during the lockdown of Covid and it became a favorite for both the kids and their parents. It gave Mom and Dad a few minutes to get something done. After a while, the grandkids started requesting favorite books to be read. This can become a good bedtime routine or a break for when Mom or Dad has to get dinner on the table. If the kids are older, read a book that they have a copy of at home, so they can follow along with you.

2. Video a tour of your house

If the circumstances of your life mean that your grandchildren have not yet been able to visit you, why not record a tour of your house and yard? Show them where you eat dinner and where you sleep. What room do you sit in when you call them? Make a video of that room and one of your kitchen. It is so much easier to visualize someone in your mind if you can also see, in your head, their surroundings. An added plus is if they are able to visit you in the future, they'll feel comfortable in your home, because they already know it.

3. Send them on a scavenger hunt

Make a list of things for them to find. If they are able to go outside in their yard while you are on the phone with them, you can have them look for leaves, rocks, stones or twigs. If you play this game while they are indoors, ask them to find a bear or a lion or whatever stuffed animal you know they have. Or you can have them look for something red or green. It's all about the interaction.

4. A day in the life

Pick a day at random and have the kids, or the parents, take photos of their daily activities: eating a meal, playing with siblings, waiting for the school bus, going to the store, or getting ready for bed. The sky is the limit on this one. Have them send you the photos via email or text so that you can print them up to make a small photo album of the day. The bonus is that on that same day you do the same thing! Take photos of you having breakfast or going to lunch with friends or reading a book; whatever it is you do. Then you send them the pictures the same way. Print these also to include in your mini album. In fact, make two albums. When you do get together, you can bring one album along and gift it as a surprise.

For Teens

Your teenage grandchildren are busy. School, after-school activities, friends, maybe a job, homework, family life, pressure, all add to their stress. You don't want to be an additional chore on their "to do" list.

Permit them take the lead. Their world is text, Whats App, FaceTime, Snapchat, etc. The number one complaint I hear from teens in regards to keeping in touch with their grandparents is that *Grandma wants to talk for an hour!* Trust me, they don't have a spare hour to chit chat.

Don't expect long flowing conversations. While they would love to include you in their already over-scheduled and busy world, it has to be in short bursts. A text wishing them well on a test, or a simple *Good morning honey. I'm thinking of you today* or *Good Luck on your track meet* will go a long way to building a continuing relationship. They won't be in high school forever and your efforts in building a relationship should pay off big time when they are young adults.

If they feel that you respect them and their communication style now, when they do have free time they'll want to seek you out to spend time with you.

When you are able to talk to them for more than 10

seconds, ask questions that require a thoughtful answer. Don't ask them *how was school today*, because you already know that the answer is going to be *fine.*

Instead ask them questions that will give you insight to their day-to-day lives. *Do you prefer to sit in the front or the back of the class? Do you have a favorite teacher? What do you like about him/her? Which class do you love to go to? Which one do you dislike? Is it because of the teacher or the subject matter?*

Show an interest in whatever subject is that they love to learn. You might be surprised that the preschooler who loved to build castles when he was young now prefers to paint murals. Or the little girl who couldn't stop moving when she was a preschooler can sit quietly and play chess for hours.

After you've asked the question, button your lip. Listen to them as you refrain from butting in to give unsolicited and unwanted advice.

Allow them to answer with as little or as much information that they are willing to share.

Keep an open mind and don't fall back on the *When I was your age* conversation. Because things were completely different for us when we were their age. You can't, and shouldn't even if you could, solve their problems for them. They need to learn how to handle sticky situations on their own. Your role now is to be supportive.

And when they tell you that it's time for them to hang up, let them!

Here are other ways to interact with your long-distance teen.

1. Write your family history

You don't have to be a pro to write an anecdote or a paragraph about your family history. Write a memory to send to your teen. It could be one from your childhood or a memory of your children growing up (especially if you write one about your son/daughter who's now their father/mother). Or you can write a memory about your grandkids when they were little or how you felt the first time you held them in your arms. If you are intimidated when it comes to filling a blank page, think of a memory and jot it down on a large index card. It doesn't have to be an essay. Send one each time you mail them a card or letter. You'll be surprised at how easy it is and how cherished those written memories become.

2. "Open when" letters or cards

This is good for all ages, but will be especially appreciated by teens. Whenever there is an upcoming milestone in their future, write an encouraging note about it and send it a few weeks early. On the back of the envelope, write the day/date that they should open the card. *Open when you pass your driving test. Open when the recital/play/game is over. Open on the last day of the school year. Open on the night before your first day of junior year. Open on your 15th birthday.* You get the idea. The joy is in the sense of anticipation which comes from receiving a note, card or letter.

3. Play games together online

There's an abundance of online game sites which allow you to play one-on-one board games, like chess or checkers. Take the time to do a Google search for a few websites to see what games might best suit you and your teen grandchildren.

Or do a Google search for apps which have games that are familiar to grandparents; games like Monopoly, Uno, and dominoes. And if your grandchild wants you to learn some new, interactive video games, take up the challenge and try it.

Some Near, Some Far

If you have grandchildren who live nearby and another brood living far away, it can be heart-wrenching. By virtue of proximity, it's easier to establish a bond with the children who live nearby. Here are some suggestions that can help you bridge the gap.

1. Include the long-distance ones in family functions whenever possible

This can be a delicate situation, because some children, due to age or temperament, might not be able to handle seeing their cousins having so much fun with Grandma and Grandpa when they themselves can't be there. But if they do have the right temperament, try to incorporate them in the activity even if they can't be there physically.

For example, even though you know that there is no way that the long-distance children can be part of a local activity, send them an invitation anyway to allow them to feel included. If you are able to get the cousins to Skype or FaceTime for a few minutes during the celebration, that would be great. And when the activity is over, send the far away kids any little party favors or photos to commemorate the event.

2. Teach them a skill

Remember in the previous chapter where I discussed teaching a skill to your local grandchild? It's easy to teach a skill to the grandchildren that live near you. But what can you do for your grandchildren who live far away?

You can instruct and teach via FaceTime or a livestream like Google Duo. It works on YouTube, so it can work for us. Can you bake? Notify them in advance what recipe you will use and what ingredients and supplies they are going to need and set up a time to bake banana bread or muffins or whatever it is you like to bake.

Other skills that are easy to teach are crochet and knitting. Make sure they have the minimal supplies and show them how to chain or cast on.

Are you an artist? If not, why not? As Picasso said, "Every child is an artist. The problem is how to remain an artist once we grow up." So why not do a paint along? You'll have as much fun as they do. And if your artistic vibes dissipated as you grew up, here is a golden opportunity to develop them once again and awaken your inventive spirit.

Another possibility is to plant a pack of seeds together. Send them a package with a small pot, the seeds, a little bit of soil, and a children's sized gardening set, which you can get on Amazon for under $10. Plant the seeds together at the same time and share the joy of watching both plants blossom in a weekly call.

3. Mad Libs

Remember Mad Libs? I've never met a child yet who doesn't get into a giggling fit over Mad Libs. You can buy the books and do one page each time you speak to your grandchild. Or, if you prefer, you can go to madlibs.com for printable pages.

4. Read books to them with cliffhanger chapter endings

There are quite a few fun and fabulous book series available that will leave your child eagerly anticipating the next chapter. *The Magic Treehouse* books is one great example. Be sure to read this series in order since each book refers to a portion of the story in the previous book. Another good choice is the *Choose Your Own Adventure* books. Each time you connect with your grandchild, let them choose which page he prefers to continue on his adventure for the next reading. *Harry Potter* or *The Little House on the Prairie* books will keep you going for a long time as well.

5. Eat dinner together (virtually)

During the beginning days of Covid, Alan Alda would have dinner virtually with other couples via Zoom. Why not do the same with your family? Schedule a day that works for both families and sit down at the table and share a virtual meal.

6. Treat each child as the individual he/she is

What this means is your grandchildren will quite likely not all be in the same age group. You may have a 12-year-old girl, an 11-year-old boy, an eight-year-old boy, and a two-year-old girl.

Try not to lump the 12-year-old-girl and an eight-year-old boy in the same category simply because they happen to be siblings. They are individuals with individual tastes and interests. Go the extra mile by personalizing things for them. Correspond with them according to their age and style preference and send each of them things that are appropriate for their age and interest.

That being said, if you have a few grandchildren who

are several years apart in age, you might consider doing a virtual simple craft activity where the older ones can assist the younger ones. There is no one-size-fits all and it's okay to try several things to see what works best.

If a grandchild has a particular passion, encourage them to teach you what they know. One kid who is interested in art may enjoy giving you a virtual art lesson, while another learning a musical instrument might want to share how to play scales. Be open to them.

Chapter Seven

My Final Suggestion

If you are at all able to, take each individual grandchild on a week-long trip (or even just a weekend) on a special adventure.

This might not be doable for a number of reasons. Time, money, health, physical limitations, logistics, and/or the number of grandchildren you have can make this final suggestion difficult for you.

But if it is at all possible, I highly recommend giving this one a chance.

I've had contemporaries take one granddaughter to Israel for a family wedding and then a year later, take her sibling, their grandson, to the opposite coast for a week-long excursion of whale watching and airplane museum visits.

If you can't swing a longer trip for any number of reasons, can you take one grandchild at a time on a relatively close overnight excursion? For example, I had a friend whose kindergarten age grandchild's biggest wish was to stay in a hotel for a day or two. The grandparents booked a hotel in their own town and they gave him his dream trip. He got to swim in the pool, eat breakfast in bed while watching TV, had dinner at a diner and stay up past his bedtime. That may not sound like a huge deal to you or me, but to a five-year-old it was the vacation of a lifetime.

There you have it. I hope that you'll discover things in this book that will enrich your relationship with all of your grandchildren. Peruse it as each season of their lives change and engage with them by trying out as many activities that your personal situation allows. It all goes so fast.

If you take the time and put in the effort you will be rewarded a thousand times over. You will find that you and your grandchildren will be *Forever Connected*.

About the author

I'm an award-winning columnist, author, editor and writing teacher, who has dedicated my professional career to the art of making writing fun. My writings appear in a variety of publications, including *Boys' Life, Christian Home and School, Readers' Digest, Chicken Soup for the Soul,* and *Christian Science Monitor*, as well as in many state standardized testing books, including *Measuring Up to the New York State Learning Standards* and *Measuring Up to the Texas Essential Knowledge and Skills*, among others.

A selection of books that I have recently published on KDP Amazon and which are geared towards young children and school-age kids include:

-The Whimsical Animal Book of Wacky Rhymes
-The Awesome True Story of Oddey the Owl: A Heartwarming Story of Survival
-50 Writing Prompts Activity Book for Your 2nd Grader
-The 50 Writing Prompts Workbook for Your 3rd Grader
-199 Fun Writing Prompts for 4th and 5th Graders
-200 Fun Writing Prompts for Your 6th, 7th and 8th Graders

-Writing Prompts for Kids: Thought-Provoking Prompts Based on Quotes from History's Most Famous and Influential Thinkers
-College Application Essay Tips: Do's and Don'ts for a Powerful and Convincing Admissions Essay

I had the pleasure of raising three young boys, who have since grown into three young men, and who have given me the beautiful gift of grandparenthood.

If you've enjoyed this book, please consider posting an Amazon review. I'm always happy to hear your comments and suggestions.

Click here or scan the QR code below to leave your honest review.

SCAN HERE

Made in United States
Troutdale, OR
04/26/2024